EVERYDAY GRACES

STORIES OF FAITH IN THE ORDINARY

C.E. ALBANESE

GNAW BONE PUBLISHING, LLC

A NOTE ON GRACE

Grace is one of the most beautiful and foundational truths of Christian faith. At its heart, grace is the free and undeserved gift of God's love. It manifests in both the monumental and the mundane, often revealing itself most powerfully in the everyday moments we might otherwise overlook.

In small things, grace may arrive as a neighbor's unexpected kindness, the memory of a loved one just as loneliness closes in, or a forgotten photograph resurfacing when you need to remember that you belong.

Grace in the big things tends to be more dramatic, but no less mysterious: the strength to serve when your pride urges you to rebel, the capacity to love in moments of profound loss, or a chance at reconciliation when hope feels nearly gone.

What's remarkable is how small and large graces often interweave, reminding us that we're not entirely self-sufficient—that something beyond us is quietly at work, bending the world toward healing and wholeness.

The challenge is developing our senses to recognize this divine gift, whether in the crisis that transforms everything, or in the ordinary Tuesday that somehow feels touched by something sacred.

Perhaps, then, the stories that follow aren't merely stories, but invitations—quiet whispers that grace is always near, waiting to be noticed in the glint of the ordinary and the shimmer of the sacred.

Although this is presented as fiction, you'll find me in several of the stories. Hopefully, you'll find yourself too.

SERVING HANDS

Lucas slouched in the pew, arms crossed, as he watched Father Don pour water over some old woman's feet, gently washing her swollen ankles and toes.

Gross, Lucas thought, checking his phone for the third time. *And weird.*

His dad shot him a look that could've melted steel. Lucas pocketed the phone and straightened, but his mind wandered to the playoff game he was missing, to the group chat blowing up without him.

"This is what Jesus did for his disciples," Father Don said, drying the woman's feet with a white towel. "He showed them that to lead is to serve. And to serve is to love."

Lucas rolled his eyes. *Yeah, right. Washing feet means you're the boss now? Sounds more like punishment.*

The ceremony dragged on—more feet, more water, more towels. Relieved he dodged being selected, Lucas counted ceiling tiles, studied the stained glass, anything to avoid watching the uncomfortable spectacle of grownups touching each other's feet.

Finally, mercifully, Mass ended.

The ride home was quiet except for the radio playing some oldies station. Lucas stared out the window, planning his PlayStation escape.

At home, they found Grandpa Tony perched on the edge of his recliner, wrestling with his compression socks.

Lucas started toward the stairs, already thinking of the login screen of his favorite game, when something made him pause. His grandfather's feet—swollen, pale—looked just like the old woman's in church.

To serve is to love.

The words came back unbidden. Lucas had rolled his eyes at them an hour ago, but watching his grandfather's quiet struggle, they didn't sound quite so ridiculous.

Lucas found himself moving toward the recliner before his father could offer help. Without thinking, he dropped to his knees beside his grandfather's chair, remembering the white towel in Father Don's hands.

"Here, Pop, let me."

Lucas' hands were steady as he guided the sock over his grandfather's swollen foot, careful around the spots where diabetes had left dark marks on his skin. The compression fabric was stubborn, but Lucas worked patiently, the way he'd seen Father Don work with the towel.

When he looked up, his grandfather's eyes glistened.

"Thank you, son," Grandpa Tony whispered, his voice thick. "You've got good hands. Gentle hands."

Lucas felt something shift in his chest—a tightness, then a loosening. "Yeah," he said quietly, still kneeling. "No problem, Pop."

Later that night while lying in bed, Lucas couldn't stop thinking about his grandfather's tears, about how small the act had been and how much it had meant. He pulled out his phone and searched "Holy Thursday foot washing."

Love means service: not punishment.

Lucas read it twice, then set his phone on his chest and stared at the ceiling.

He got it now.

SMALL FAVORS

*J*ames reached for the rooster-shaped salt shaker as his mother set a plate of scrambled eggs and buttered toast before him.

"You're going to be late for school—again."

"Relax, Ma." He popped the cork and seasoned his eggs. "It's a half day."

"That's what you said yesterday." She cleared her throat.

He caught his mother's frown mid-bite. With a sigh, he crossed himself and mumbled grace.

His mother ruffled his hair—always treating him like a little kid—then moved to the kitchen window.

A cool breeze stirred the floral curtains, bringing with it the morning sounds of the city: laundry flapping on lines strung between buildings, car horns echoing off brick walls, children's laughter rising from the alleyway.

"Rita?" His mother leaned out. "Hate to bother you, but could I borrow a pinch of salt?"

"Coming right up," called a voice from the neighboring window.

James's eyes darted from his food to his mother's back. Did he hear that right? Rita—the neighbor who was always borrowing sugar or coffee or whatever else she ran out of, who probably spent her money on those fancy flowers she kept on her windowsill instead of groceries—was actually giving instead of taking?

James watched his mother stretch out her hand. "Thanks, Rita, you're a lifesaver." She pulled the curtains closed and returned to the table, setting Rita's shaker beside the rooster.

He stared at the two shakers—theirs proud and decorative, Rita's worn smooth.

"Ma, why'd you do that?" He nodded toward the miniature rooster. "We've got plenty."

"Rita's husband hurt his back a few months ago and hasn't been able to work. They've been borrowing things here and there. So sometimes, I ask her for little things I know she can spare." Her voice softened. "When you let someone help you, it tells them they matter."

James's throat tightened and the eggs turned to ash in his mouth. He pushed back from the table and snatched Rita's shaker. "I'll give it back on my way to school."

His mother smiled. "Look at that—running late and still making time to help a neighbor. Maybe there's hope for you yet."

James grabbed his bookbag and Rita's shaker, dipped his head to hide his smile, then hurried out the door.

GRACE BEFORE DINNER

*J*ulie felt her mother's wedding ring press against her palm as they joined hands around the kitchen table. Five years, and Mom still wore it. Five years to the day since the anniversary dinner Dad had planned at that little Italian place downtown he loved—before the heart attack took him.

To her right, ten-year-old Zoe's fingers were sticky from sneaking bites of mashed potatoes. Julie squeezed gently, and Zoe squeezed back—their little signal that meant *I love you* in their mother-daughter wordless language.

"Bless us, O Lord, and these thy gifts," her mother began, her Midwestern accent sneaking through, along with a tremor that Julie felt through their clasped hands.

Her phone buzzed from the counter where she'd deliberately left it. Ron's third call today. She'd seen her husband's name flash across the screen during dinner prep and let it go to voicemail. Just like the other two.

"...which we are about to receive from thy bounty..."

Thoughts of Ron surfaced, followed by that familiar knot of resentment. Twenty years in the Army, and he'd already made general. The promotion was supposed to be a good thing—they'd agreed on that. But twelve months of him on the other side of the country felt infinite when measured in bedtime stories read alone, soccer games where she cheered for two, and Zoe's questions about why Daddy couldn't just come home for dinner like other dads. *He chose this*, she thought bitterly. *He could have said no. He knew they couldn't go with him.*

The base housing had seemed too cramped anyway, Zoe's school here was excellent, and her mother needed them close. All sound reasons that felt flimsy at three a.m., when the bed stretched empty beside her.

"...through Christ our Lord..."

"And please keep Mr. Tumbles safe," Zoe whispered, just loud enough for the prayer to catch it. "His nose was warm today, and this YouTuber says that's bad for hamsters."

Julie's mother's lip twitched—the first real expression she'd shown all evening. Even in grief, she couldn't resist her granddaughter's earnestness.

"Amen," they said together.

But none of them let go right away. Zoe because she never did, always trying to stretch every family moment longer. Mom because anniversaries made everything feel fragile. And Julie because—

She looked at their joined hands. Her mother clinging to love five years gone. Zoe, holding tight to whatever family she could reach. Both of them choosing connection over protection, choosing to stay open despite the hurt.

And here she was, letting Ron's calls go unanswered because she was angry. Withholding what they both needed most.

"Amen," she whispered again, but this time Julie squeezed both hands tighter.

Dinner was getting cold, but grace held them a moment longer. When they finally let go, Julie quietly slipped her phone into her pocket.

NO DESSERT DADDY

Omar pushed away the plate of chocolate chip cookies, still warm from the oven. "Not for me, thanks."

His wife Jocell raised an eyebrow. "Where's my husband and what have you done with him?"

"Lent," he said, settling back in his chair. "Giving up sweets for forty days. Good discipline, and a little self-control should help me lose some weight."

Six-year-old Mason looked up from his coloring book, cookie crumbs dotting his chin. "Why can't Daddy have cookies?"

"Daddy's fasting," Jocell explained. "It's how we pray with our bodies." She wiped Mason's face. "Daddy also needs to get rid of that big tummy before people start thinking he's Santa."

Mason giggled. Omar doubted that his son understood fasting, but the Santa joke clearly landed.

The first week zipped past. Omar felt virtuous watching his family enjoy dessert while he sipped coffee. This Lent thing's a breeze.

But by week two, the smell of Jocell's banana bread made his mouth water. At work, he watched colleagues demolish a birthday cake while he ate an apple. Still, he held strong.

Wednesday of the third week, Mason climbed into his lap after dinner, clutching half a chocolate pudding cup.

"What's that for, buddy?"

"For you, Daddy." He held it out. "For after Easter when you can have treats again."

Omar's throat tightened. "Mason, you don't have to—"

"I want to wait with you, Daddy."

Jocell appeared in the doorway, watching quietly.

That night, Omar found a container in the fridge labeled DADDY'S TREATS in Mason's wobbly handwriting. Inside: half a cookie, gummy bears, two Hershey kisses.

"He's been saving them from his school lunch," Jocell whispered. "Keeps saying Daddy will be so hungry when Lent ends."

Omar stared at the container. His discipline suddenly felt selfish, small. He'd focused on his own willpower, his own spiritual growth. But Mason had turned his fast into an act of love.

The next evening, as Mason wrapped half his brownie in a napkin, Omar knelt beside his chair.

"You know what? I think Jesus likes it better when we give things up together."

Mason tilted his head.

"How about we both skip dessert sometimes? And buy food for people who don't have enough?"

Mason's face lit up. "Like a team?" he asked.

"Exactly like a team."

That Sunday, they walked hand-in-hand to the food pantry, carrying groceries. Mason insisted on carrying the cake mix himself.

"This is better than saving my cookies," he announced.

Omar squeezed his small hand. "Much better, buddy. Much better."

UNEXPECTED GIFT

Early summer light filtered through oak leaves as Carl and Sheila walked Bella through their quiet neighborhood. The border collie's tail wagged, alert to every rustling bush.

As they rounded the corner onto Maple Street, they spotted Mr. Lee in his driveway, hunched over his ancient lawn mower, cigarette dangling. The elderly Chinese man was a familiar sight—always tending his immaculate yard with monastic devotion.

"Looks like he needs a hand," Sheila said.

Carl pretended he didn't hear the comment. Getting involved in someone else's lawn care was the last thing he wanted to do. A cold beer, a comfy couch, and the last few innings of the Nats game waited for him back home.

"Carl!" Mr. Lee called out, his voice carrying the careful cadence of someone translating thoughts before speaking. "You help? Please?"

Carl felt his wife's finger poke his side.

With a sigh, he approached, Bella sniffing curiously at the oil-stained pavement.

"Engine no start," Mr. Lee explained, wiping his hands on a faded cloth. "I pull, pull—nothing." He mimed tugging the cord, then huffed.

"Very old. Like me, yes?" His crooked finger pointed to the engine. "You look. Okay?"

Carl nodded as he knelt and examined the machine. The mower looked just as worn and tired as its owner—rust blooming along its edges, pull cord frayed beyond repair. Carl checked the gas, the dipstick, tugged the starter. The engine coughed and sputtered. Another yank, harder. The cord snapped.

"I don't think this one's coming back, Mr. Lee," Carl said, stepping back.

The old man's shoulders sagged.

"I've got an electric mower at home," Carl offered. "Let me bring it over."

Mr. Lee's eyes widened, then he nodded gratefully.

Sheila and Bella waited as Carl rushed home. Five minutes later, he returned, pushing a sleek electric mower.

Tears pooled in Mr. Lee's dark eyes as he hobbled forward.

Without warning, the reserved man wrapped him in a fierce hug. Carl froze—they'd only ever exchanged polite waves. Now Mr. Lee was embracing him like family.

"Thank you, thank you," Mr. Lee whispered, voice thick with emotion.

"The battery's charged, so you're all set," Carl said, demonstrating the simple start button.

"Charger?" Mr. Lee asked hopefully. "For next time?"

Carl paused. Mr. Lee wasn't asking to borrow—he thought this was a gift. *Should I correct him? Attempt to navigate the awkward translation? Or...*

Mr. Lee's face radiated with gratitude and joy.

"I'll go get it for you," Carl said quietly, and gestured to Sheila.

Walking home, his wife squeezed his arm. "We're buying another mower after the game, aren't we?"

Carl smiled. "Yup."

BEADS AND BREAKS

The minivan's tires screeched as it swerved back into the lane, past a row of mailboxes. Jason gritted his teeth and punched the gas—he wasn't losing again. The four-cylinder engine whined, coughed, then sputtered. The other car's taillights shrank in the distance—and with it, high school bragging rights slipped away.

A second later, red and blue lights lit up behind him. The siren came next.

"Idiot," Jason muttered, slamming the dash as he pulled over. His heart pounded harder than it had during the race. His mom's voice echoed in his head: *Drive like someone's life depends on it, because it might.*

The officer's door opened. Jason stared straight ahead, hands glued to ten and two—as if it mattered now. A glance in the sideview mirror.

Officer Froller.

Jason's stomach dropped.

Froller swept his flashlight beam through the interior, then tapped on the window. Jason lowered the glass.

"License and registration."

Jason nodded, fumbling. He popped open the glove compartment

—and a tangle of rosary beads spilled out. His mom's old wooden set. The crucifix clinked against the console.

They both stared at it for a beat.

"Saw your parents at church the other day," Froller said, "Haven't seen you for months." He held out his hand for the papers.

Jason handed over the documents. He tried to think of a reply, something Mom would've expected him to say. All he managed was a dry "Sorry."

"Bet you are." Froller glanced up the road. "You racing?"

Jason didn't answer.

"Thought so." Froller stepped back, hands resting on his belt. Jason heard him sigh but kept still.

"I'm not writing you a ticket tonight," Froller said. "You deserve it —and then some." He returned the paperwork. "But tell you what—I see you in church next Sunday with your parents, we'll call this even."

Jason nodded, swallowing hard. "Yes, sir. You will."

Froller started to walk away, then paused. "Pick those up. They've been doing more protecting than you realize."

The rosary lay against the floor mat as if they'd been waiting there. Jason reached down, coiled the beads carefully, and slipped them into his jacket pocket.

He drove home slower than he had since getting his license, fingers brushing the crucifix at every stoplight.

ICE CREAM 911

Officer Keenan's radio crackled. "Dispatch to one-o-six."

Keenan unclipped his mic, eyes still focused on the road. "Go for one-o-six."

"Respond to 39 Chesterfield for welfare check involving a juvenile. Young boy called to report his mother ate his ice cream, then hung up."

Keenan cocked his head, clicked his radio. "One-o-six—you kidding me, dispatch?"

"Negative. Sarge wants you to make sure everything's okay."

"Copy, en route," Keenan replied, and made a U-turn at the next intersection.

Five minutes later, he pulled up to a cookie-cutter two-story home —overgrown lawn, newer model minivan in the driveway, American flag hanging limp by the front door.

He rang the bell. Footsteps. The door swung open.

A young woman in pajamas, tired eyes, holding an infant to her chest. "Oh my..." Her eyes widened. "He actually called you."

Keenan cleared his throat. "We received a 911 call, ma'am. I'm here to make sure everyone's okay."

The mother looked equal parts embarrassed and exhausted.

She glanced up the adjacent staircase. "Robbie!" Her voice was tight but firm. "Get your butt down here—this instant!"

Keenan peered inside. Pots and pans covered the kitchen island, dishes lined the counter. Kids toys littered the living room where a cartoon played on the TV.

A little boy leaped down the stairs, his five-year-old face set in an old man's scowl.

"Young man, if your father was home—"

"He would've stopped you from eating my ice cream!" The boy stood on the bottom step, arms crossed tight. "That's stealing! Daddy says stealing is bad and you go to jail."

The mom glanced at Keenan. "My husband's National Guard, gone for two weeks." She slumped against the door. "It's been a long day."

Keenan nodded. Twenty years in the Guard himself—he knew about those annual training requirements and the stress it had placed on his wife and kids. He made eye contact with the little boy and put on his "dad" voice. "Did you call 911, Robbie?"

"I told Siri to call. Mommy ate my ice cream and needs to go to jail for it." His face softened, his arms fell to his side. "But I don't want that anymore. I just wanted *my* chocolate-chip cone."

"Well," Keenan said, crouching down, "your mom's not going to jail. But maybe we can work something out."

That evening, Keenan returned with a half-gallon of ice cream, waffle cones, and rainbow sprinkles.

Robbie's eyes went wide. "This for me?"

"For both of you," Keenan said, glancing at the exhausted mom. "But next time you need help, call the non-emergency number, okay? I'll still come over."

As he walked back to his cruiser, Keenan heard Robbie through the open window: "Mommy, you can have some of mine." The words echoed something his old chaplain during his Guard days used to say about the loaves and fishes—how grace multiplied when shared, even by the smallest hands.

LOST AND FOUND

Jimmy tossed the designer pillow, yanked off the comforter. The Egyptian cotton sheets were next. *Where the heck is it?* He'd slipped it from his wrist before getting in the shower, positive he'd left it on the bed.

"Hey, hun." He made sure his voice carried downstairs. "Did you move my dad's watch?"

"No," came her reply, followed by the television volume rising.

Jimmy dropped to his knees, running his hands under the bed frame. Nothing. His breath quickened. The Timex with the cracked leather band—Dad had worn it through Vietnam and every one of Jimmy's Little League games.

A glance at the expensive sheets and comforter piled on the floor—another mess he'd have to explain later. A sigh built in his chest. Then, almost automatically, an old prayer.

"Saint Anthony, Saint Anthony, please come around." The words flowed from memory. "Something's lost and can't be found."

Something pulled him toward the nightstand. The drawer rattled open, revealing loose papers yellowed with age, bills that should've been tossed years ago. No watch.

As if it would've been that easy.

Before slamming the drawer shut, a flash of white and plastic caught his eye—a faded Polaroid.

Him and Mike as kids, Jimmy's arm slung over his little brother's shoulder, both grinning at the camera. They'd been inseparable once, but distance and resentment had carved a canyon between them. Mike had stayed, turned down that job with Delta, caring for Mom and Dad as they declined. Jimmy had chased success in the city—big job, big money, bigger ego.

When Mom died, Dad followed a month later. Nothing left but memories and one battered watch. The watch Mike had wanted. The watch Dad had left to Jimmy. And the rift that ensued.

His phone rang, bringing his thoughts back to the present. Another telemarketer. A tap ended it before the pitch began.

Still clutching the photo, Jimmy scrolled to his brother's contact, hesitated, then pressed call.

"Hello?" Mike's voice, cautious.

Awkward silence stretched. Jimmy paced, nervous energy carrying him into the bathroom. He stopped midstride.

There it was—Dad's Timex, right where he'd left it, patient as always.

"Hey, Mikey." Jimmy's voice cracked slightly. "I was wondering... you want to grab a bite sometime?" He rubbed the watch's face. "I've gotten something that belongs to you."

A pause. Then, softer: "Yeah, Jimmy, I'd like that... I'd like that a lot."

HEARTS AND GRADES

Mike opened the door to the mudroom. Behind him, the Jeep's engine fan spun wildly, like a dying animal, then went quiet. Another twelve-hour day behind him, and his car was probably dying too. Before he could drop his bag and slip off his shoes, he heard Haley scolding Lizzy—again.

Their voices were muffled, but not Lizzy's shriek. And not the door slamming upstairs.

He glanced over his shoulder, keys dangling from his fingers. Then, with a sigh, he shut the garage door and entered the kitchen.

Two steps in he spotted the broken ceramic scattered across the tile. His favorite mug. The lopsided one that Lizzy made in third grade. *World's Best Dad* scrawled in purple crayon glaze.

Haley stood at the sink, gripping the counter's edge, her back rigid.

"Do I need to report a murder?" he asked, crouching to collect the larger pieces.

Her spine stiffened. The joke didn't land. They never did.

"Your daughter failed her history final," she said, back still turned. "And her algebra one."

"Oh." The ceramic shards dug into his palm. Lizzy was never *their daughter* when she messed up.

"I asked you to study with her." Haley whipped around, face scrunched. She nodded at the broken mug. "Yeah, she did that too."

"I've got it," he said, standing.

Upstairs, muffled music seeped under Lizzy's door. He knocked twice, then entered.

She was pressed against the wall, knees to her chest, eyes red-rimmed. Used tissues circled her feet like fallen rose petals. Above her desk, her First Communion photo caught the afternoon light.

"Hey, kiddo." He sat on the bed's edge. "Rough day?"

"I'm sorry about your mug, Dad. My backpack caught it when I—" Her voice cracked. "I know I messed up the tests too."

He wanted to ask about studying. About priorities. But something in her expression stopped him.

"What's going on, Lizzy?"

Fresh tears spilled over.

"There's this boy at school. Tyler. We were... talking. Then today he told everyone I was ugly and weird and—"

She gulped air.

His chest tightened. He didn't even know she liked someone. She was only thirteen—too young for this heartbreak, right? But he remembered being her age. Stealing his first kiss after Sunday school.

He dropped to the floor, placing his hand on her knee. "I'm sorry that happened, sweetheart."

A minute passed. Then another, and another.

Feet shuffled in the hallway. Haley appeared with two steaming mugs. He saw her posture was softer now, eyes tired but kind. She placed the mugs next to the photo, then kissed Lizzy's forehead—a benediction. "Boys are dumb." She gestured at him, winked. "Even your father sometimes."

"We'll email your teachers tomorrow," he said gently. "See about retaking those tests."

Lizzy looked up, surprised. "Really?"

"Really." He squeezed her shoulder. "Hearts heal. Grades can too."

SHARED SLICE

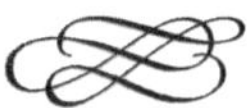

Cliff shoved through the lunch crowd at Tony Brothers Pizza, phone buzzing with a text from his boss. *Guess it's a working lunch.*

The old-school checkered tablecloths and vintage Coca-Cola signs blurred past as he scanned for a table. There was a line out the door, as usual. That's what made this place worth it.

A two-seat table by the window opened up. Perfect. He shouldered past a young couple—purple hair, face piercings, neck tattoos. *Kids these days.*

He dropped into the metal chair, laptop open before he'd even settled. Another message from his boss popped up—the quarterly reports needed revision. Again.

"What can I get ya?" The waitress appeared, looking frazzled.

"Personal pan pizza, your special, and a Coke," Cliff said, fingers already flying across the keyboard.

She nodded and disappeared.

An old man slid into the seat across from him—worn flannel, gray stubble, that unmistakable smell of someone living rough. Cliff's jaw tightened. *Great.*

The old man slid a stack of paper napkins across the table.

Cliff wrinkled his nose. "I'm fine, thanks." He turned back to his screen, shaking his head. *Probably gonna ask for a buck next.*

Minutes later, the waitress returned with a steaming pizza, setting it between them and hurrying away.

Cliff grabbed a slice without looking, balancing his laptop with one hand while he ate. The old man took a slice too. Cliff caught the act from the corner of his eye. *Seriously?*

The old man took a second slice. Then a third.

By the time Cliff finished his piece, only one slice remained. He reached out. The old man did too, but pulled back with a small smile. Cliff hesitated for just a moment. Then he took it anyway, eating quickly to avoid eye contact.

The waitress reappeared with another pizza.

"Sorry for the delay," she said, setting it in front of Cliff. "We're slammed."

Cliff stared at the fresh pie, then at the empty pan in front of the old man.

His order had just arrived. Which meant...

He glanced at the old man, who was quietly wiping his hands with one of the napkins he'd offered earlier.

Cliff's stomach dropped. Somewhere deep down, he'd known all along.

"Why didn't you say anything?" he asked, his voice barely above a whisper.

"You looked stressed and hungry." The old man smiled gently. "A combo I know all too well."

Cliff closed his laptop, searching for a reply.

"I had one of those jobs, too," the old man said. "And I missed a lot of lunches because of it." He wiped his mouth. "Missed my family too."

When the waitress returned, Cliff quietly asked for both checks.

LOVE IN THE MOMENT

George stared at his untouched breakfast. The dining room buzzed around him. Couples planned their day over coffee. Families debated which castles to visit. He kept his eyes down, cutting his eggs into smaller and smaller pieces.

The river cruise had been Margaret's dream—vineyards and castles, cobblestone streets and cathedral bells. They'd talked about it for years, always putting it off. *Next summer. When we retire.*

A groan grew in his chest. He hated boats. Always had. Margaret was the one who loved the water, loved people, loved turning everything into an adventure. Now he was here alone, wondering what the heck he was doing.

Behind him, a young couple argued, loud—something about missing a tour, about him always being on his phone, about her tight schedule.

"I'm going for a walk," the woman snapped, pushing her chair back.

As she stormed past George, something small and silver slipped from her wrist, skittering across the deck and rolling to a stop at his feet.

He bent slowly, knees protesting, and picked it up. A bracelet. The inscription on the charm caught the sunlight: *Live in the Moment.*

His breath caught. Margaret's voice rose in his mind, gentle but insistent: *Don't just live in the moment, George. Love in the moment.*

The woman was almost out of sight. George looked back at the young man still glued to his phone.

"Miss!" he called out, shuffling after her.

She whipped around, still flushed with anger.

"You dropped this." He held out the bracelet.

"Oh." Her expression softened. "Thank you."

George fiddled with his wedding ring—Margaret's ring, still on his finger after two years.

"Miss?"

She paused. "Yeah?"

"It may not be my place..." His voice was quiet but carried. "But your bracelet's all wrong."

"Excuse me?"

"I mean—it should say *love* in the moment. My Margaret used to say that at least once a day. I didn't really understand it until... well."

She glanced at the bracelet in her palm, then back at him. Her eyes flicked to his ring.

"How long were you married?" she asked softly.

"Not long enough," he said, voice catching. "She passed two years ago."

The woman was quiet for a moment, fingers closing around the charm.

"Thank you," she said again. This time, the words landed deeper.

George watched her walk back toward the dining room, toward the young man who was finally looking up from his phone.

For the first time since boarding, George felt his Margaret's presence rather than her absence.

In the distance, church bells began to chime the hour.

CHOCOLATE PIÑATA

The mariachi trumpets, and Trevor's cousin Ronnie was doing his terrible impression of Uncle Rick snoring. Even Dad was cracking up—and that never happened at dinner.

"And then"—Ronnie stood, mimicking Uncle Rick's stretch—"he goes, 'Must've been the altitude!'"

Trevor laughed, but kept glancing around the Mexican restaurant —a habit Mom said he got from her. "You notice people," she'd tell him. "That's a gift, mijo." His gaze drifted to the old woman at the corner table. Her cane leaned against her chair like a faithful companion.

"Dad." Trevor nudged him. "That old lady over there—"

"Some people like eating alone," Dad said, not looking. "Probably just wants a quiet meal."

Trevor glanced around. Quiet? The restaurant was packed. Kids ran between tables. The band struck up another song.

The woman's enchiladas arrived. She ate slowly, eyes flicking between the kitchen and front door. Waiting for her husband? Children?

Trevor's tamales sat untouched. Dad was probably right. But

something about the way the woman stared at her plate, the careful way she sipped her water—like she was making the meal last. His stomach knotted.

"I'll be right back," he said, standing.

"Trevor—" his mom started, but he was already walking.

"Excuse me," he said, approaching the woman's table. "Are you waiting for someone?"

She looked up, eyes crinkling. "Oh, hello, sweetheart. No, no—just me tonight."

Trevor shifted, mind scrambling for something to say. Something kind, like Father Jeb might say. Nothing came.

She gestured to the empty chair. "Care to sit?"

Trevor slid in. "I'm Trevor. That's my family over there." He pointed at Ronnie, now mid-story.

"I'm Rosa," she said, setting her fork down. "And this" —she spread her arms— "is my restaurant. Twenty-five years ago today, my husband Carlos and I opened it."

Trevor's mouth fell open. "You own this place?"

"We do. Carlos is home with a cold, poor thing. First anniversary we've spent apart." She smiled. "But I couldn't stay away. Not tonight."

"That's why you're alone."

"Oh, I'm never really alone here." She nodded toward the manager. "Miguel's been with us since day one. And Sofia" —she pointed to a waitress weaving past— "fifteen years. They're mi familia. The kind you choose."

"What about your real family?" Trevor asked, then immediately felt stupid.

Rosa's laugh was warm. "Sometimes the family you choose is just as important as the one you're born into." She leaned in. "Did you order the chocolate piñata for dessert?"

Trevor shook his head. "Dad said it's too expensive."

Rosa grinned. "Tonight your bill's on the house, so tell him to order two."

Trevor stood, grinning. "Really?"

"Tu familia es mi familia tonight." She winked. "And mi familia always eats free. Now go—before that cousin of yours starts another story."

As he walked back, Rosa called to Sofia in Spanish, her voice full of joy—the kind that comes from sharing what you love most.

CHRISTMAS REGISTER

Miriam's feet ached as she unlocked the single register, the only one open in the grocery store. Christmas morning, and here she was—missing her children tearing into presents, the lazy morning in pajamas. Everything that mattered. But the overtime pay would cover Kendi's school supplies and maybe fix the washing machine.

At least they'd made it to midnight Mass together, the choir's "Silent Night" still echoing in her mind. But four hours of sleep later, she felt no peace.

The automatic doors whooshed open. An elderly man bundled against the cold shuffled in. He moved through the aisles in deadly silence.

"Good morning," Miriam offered as he approached with milk and bread.

He didn't even look up as he tapped his card against the reader.

Next a man in Christmas pajamas and a Santa hat grabbed orange juice, bacon, and pancake mix—clearly rushing back to his own family celebration.

"Merry Christmas," Miriam said, scanning the items.

"Uh-huh," he muttered, tapping his foot. "Can you hurry this up? I've got to get home."

Miriam bit her tongue and bagged his groceries in silence.

A college-age girl with dangling earbuds bought iced coffee. "Stuck working the holiday, huh?" The girl smirked. "Who'd you piss off?"

Miriam's jaw tightened. She didn't deserve this—not on Christmas. She handed over the change without a word.

By ten, the post-church rush hit. A line snaked toward produce— families grabbing forgotten ingredients, people picking last-minute gifts. All waiting for Miriam's register.

An elderly woman hobbled forward with cat food and a Snickers. Miriam scanned silently, her Christmas spirit frayed.

"You have kind eyes, dear," the woman said softly.

Miriam hesitated. *Kind?* She hadn't felt kind in hours. Still, she forced a grin as she bagged the groceries.

The woman left the candy bar, shuffling toward the exit.

Miriam grabbed the chocolate. "Ma'am, you forgot this."

"Merry Christmas, dear." Their eyes met. The woman's smile radiant, transformative.

A young father with two children stepped forward. "You know what?" He pulled a bottle of wine from his cart. "This is for you too."

The woman behind him, still in her church dress, added a roll of scratch-off lottery tickets with a warm nod.

An elderly man left a box of donuts. A little girl and her mother presented a small bouquet of flowers. One by one, the customers who had witnessed the old woman's simple gift followed her lead.

Eight hours later, Miriam stared at the pile of gifts covering her register counter. She needed a shopping cart to carry everything to her car.

In the parking lot, surrounded by unexpected abundance, she recalled the old woman's words. *Kind eyes.* Maybe that's what Christmas really was—learning to see the kindness in others, and somehow, impossibly, having them see it in you too.

THANKSGIVING TEXTS

*V*ictoria stared at the phone number on the screen. Sean. Her grandson. The silence between them stretched nearly a year—thick, bitter, and unspoken. For what? Words she'd spoken in love but delivered in judgement? Her fingers brushed the golden cross dangling from her necklace.

She opened a new text instead.

Thanksgiving dinner is at my house Nov 24, 3pm. Let me know if you're coming. Hope to see you all. Of course this includes Anna Beth & Luke.

Send.

Her phone buzzed immediately.

Who's this?

Victoria's heart sank. Had Sean deleted her number? She typed: *It's grandma. Victoria.*

Grandma? Can I have a picture

Of who?

You LOL

The casual response surprised her. Maybe Sean was ready to bridge the gap too.

Victoria opened her camera app, fumbling with the buttons until she found the front-facing camera. She adjusted her glasses, noting how the years had aged her pale face. Growing old was cruel enough. Family separation made it unbearable.

She forced a smile and snapped the photo.

In case you forgot, honey.

Send.

The response came quickly: *You not my grandma*

Victoria's heart sank. Her fingers clasped around the cross resting on her chest. Maybe she *had* waited too long. The distance now permanent. Still, she typed: *I know it's been months since we saw each other or spoke. I know your dad's still angry, but I'll always be your grandmother. Always. And I want to see you all. I miss you.*

Three dots appeared, bouncing.

Victoria held her breath, eyes fixed on those dancing dots.

A photo appeared. A young Black man in a baseball cap and AirPods, bright eyes and a goofy smile. He looked like he was in a classroom.

You not my grandma. A string of laughing emojis followed.

Victoria's face flushed with embarrassment.

Another message appeared, sandwiched in more laughing emojis: *Can I still get a plate tho? No dinner this year at my home.*

Despite everything—the family rift, the loneliness, the mortification—Victoria found herself laughing.

Of course you can. That's what grandmas do... feed everyone.

For real? You don't even know me.

Victoria hesitated for only a moment. *Sweetie, grandmas never lie. My door's open. There'll be a chair waiting. Here's the address.*

She typed out her address and hit Send.

A heart emoji appeared above her message. Then, a reply.

I'm Curtis.

Her response was automatic: *And I'm your adopted grandma.*

Another heart.

Victoria pushed back from her desk and looked out the window. For the first time in months, the heaviness in her chest lifted.

She picked up her phone again, scrolled to Sean's actual number. The unexpected conversation had stirred quiet courage. Whatever

Sean's answer, she felt lighter, ready not to just text—but talk. Her thumb hovered over the call button. "Holy Spirit," she whispered, "give me the right words." She hit call.

The phone rang once. Twice.

"Hello?" Sean's voice, uncertain.

"Hi, honey," Victoria said, surprising herself with how steady her voice sounded. "It's Grandma."

EMPTY-HANDED

The AT&T building was a ghost town. No one worked weekends during holidays—except college kids like Vinny. He settled into the guard desk with Tom Clancy's latest thriller, grateful for the quiet Christmas shift.

A few chapters in, his stomach rumbled. Book down. Lunch bag ripped open. Two PB&J sandwiches and pretzel sticks. *Yum.* His favorite. But where was his drink?

A groan.

Management had removed the vending machines during the renovation. Only water fountains now.

Four bites and the first sandwich crumbled away. The second one was in his hands when the security panel dinged.

Time to earn my seven bucks this hour.

He wolfed down the remaining wedge. Peanut butter caking the roof of his mouth, he started the patrol.

His path took him up to the fifth floor and through a galley, where the refrigerator beckoned. Inside, soda cans stood like aluminum soldiers. He eyed the smiling polar bears gracing the shiny Christmas-themed cans of Coke. His mouth instantly watered.

No one will notice.

The thought had barely finished when his hand shot out. The can burned cold against his palm.

A flick of his wrist shut the door with a thud.

He was halfway to the stairwell when the guilt hit.

What would Mom think? Sister Agnes, with her stern but kind lessons?

With a groan he returned the soda, and continued to the stairwell.

Fourth floor, same styled galley, same stacked refrigerator. He grabbed a Coke, made it ten feet, then returned it to the fridge. Again, the guilt hitting harder than the thirst.

By the third floor, he stood frozen in front of that floor's refrigerator for five full minutes, locked in moral combat. The cans stared back. His fingers twitched. The little voice on one shoulder whispered, "Do it." The voice on the other: "Don't."

He walked away empty-handed.

On the second floor, he avoided the galley entirely, stopping only at a water fountain. The flavorless liquid tasted like disappointment.

Back at the guard desk, he stared at the elevator bank. It was just a soda. Not robbery. Not grand theft. Just one lousy Coke. No one would know.

No one.

The grunt that emerged felt like gravel in his throat, but he stayed put.

Twenty minutes later, his computer screen flashed—visitors approaching. Three men in identical tan khakis and flannel shirts badged through the revolving door.

"Working weekends, huh?" Vinny said, sitting tall.

The first two smiled and passed. The third paused.

"Hey, buddy, we grabbed lunch and have an extra soda. Want it?"

Before Vinny could answer, the man set the can on his desk.

A Coke.

Same polar bears. Same Christmas design. The very one he'd held earlier.

"It's yours," the man said, then vanished around the corner with his companions.

Vinny's hands trembled as he picked the can up.
What are the odds?
He ran a finger around the rim.
Or maybe it was something more—guiding his empty hands?

AFTERWORD

These stories were born from moments when I witnessed grace break through the everyday. Sometimes in my own life, sometimes in the lives around me. A stranger's kindness. A family's quiet strength. A child's innocent prayer. Grace often arrives like that—unexpected, undeserved, but perfectly timed.

My prayer is that you, dear reader, find here a glimmer of hope. A reminder that grace is always near, waiting to touch your soul as it has mine.

—C.E. Albanese

ABOUT THE AUTHOR

C.E. Albanese is an award-winning author and former U.S. Secret Service special agent. Winner of the 2021 Clive Cussler Adventure Writers Competition Grandmaster Award, his fiction has appeared in magazines and anthologies. He co-hosts *The Crew Reviews* podcast, interviewing renowned authors. His work spans multiple genres, drawing from his faith and law enforcement background to explore authentic human experiences.

Learn more at: www.cealbanese.com